2/16

19

My Favorite Dogs

SIBERIAN HUSKY

Jinny Johnson

A+

Smart Apple Media

Published by Smart Apple Media,
an imprint of Black Rabbit Books
P.O. Box 3263, Mankato, Minnesota, 56002
www.blackrabbitbooks.com

Edited by Mary-Jane Wilkins
Designed by Hel James

Cataloging-in-Publication Data is available from the Library of Congress

ISBN 978-1-62588-179-3

Photo acknowledgements
t = top, b = bottom
title page Sirko Hartmann; 3 S-BELOV/both Shutterstock;
4-5 lvaloueva/Thinkstock; 5 aleksandr hunta/Shutterstock;
6-7 Sergey Lavrentev; 7 tarasov; 8-9 Nata Sdobnikova; 10 gillmar;
11 Dmitry Kalinovsky; 12t Andrii Ospishchev, b Eric Isselee/
all Shutterstock; 13t Denis83/Thinkstock, b Sbolotova;
14 plastique/both Shutterstock; 15t KrivoTIFF, b phetphu/
both Thinkstock; 16-17 Sirko Hartmann/Shutterstock;
18b Peter Jendrol/Thinkstock; 18-19 Pi-Lens; 20 melis;
21 Nata Sdobnikova; 22 iPics; 23 Sergey Lavrentev
Cover S-BELOV/Shutterstock

Printed in the United States of America, at Corporate Graphics
in North Mankato, Minnesota.

DAD0053a
032015
9 8 7 6 5 4 3 2

Contents

I'm a Siberian Husky!

I'm gentle, loving,
and I'm very beautiful!

I'll be your friend and I'm fun to be with. I like other dogs, too.

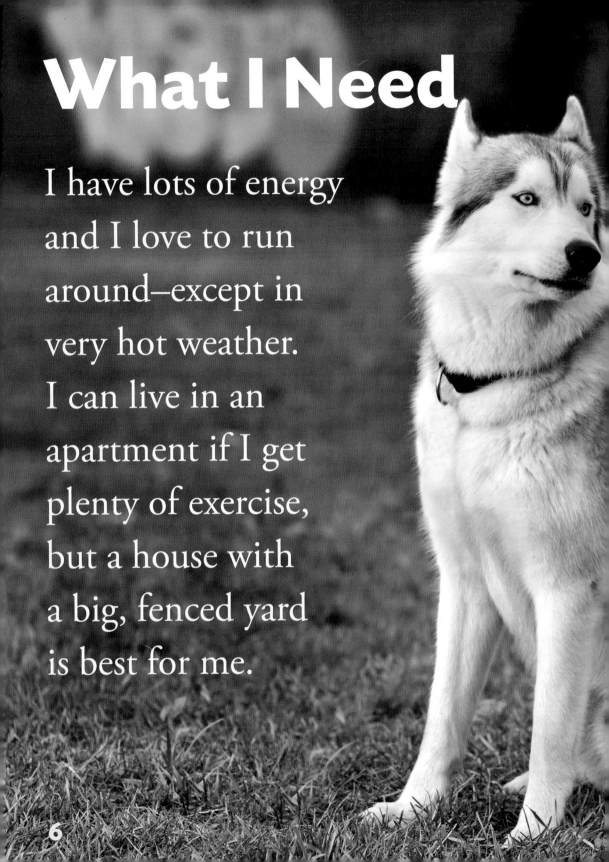

What I Need

I have lots of energy and I love to run around—except in very hot weather. I can live in an apartment if I get plenty of exercise, but a house with a big, fenced yard is best for me.

I'm really a sled dog. I'm happiest when I'm running fast in a team of dogs and pulling a sled.

I like company and I may howl if you leave me alone for long.

The Siberian Husky

Color:
All colors from
black to white

Height:
Male 21-23.5 inches
(53-60 cm);
female 20-22
inches (51-56 cm)

Weight:
Male 45-60 pounds
(20.5-27 kg);
female
35-50 pounds
(16-22.5 kg)

Double coat

Bushy
tail

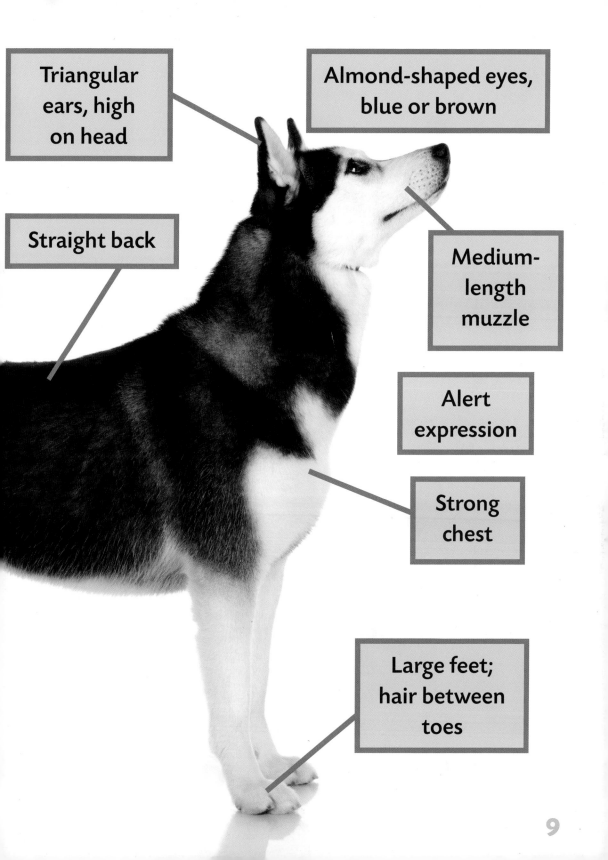

Triangular ears, high on head

Almond-shaped eyes, blue or brown

Straight back

Medium-length muzzle

Alert expression

Strong chest

Large feet; hair between toes

9

All About Siberian Huskies

The Siberian husky was bred by the Chukchi people, who live in Siberia. The dogs were used to pull sleds and herd reindeer. They were part of the family and treated as pets.

Nearly 100 years ago, people in Alaska caught a dangerous illness called diphtheria. Teams of huskies carried medicine for hundreds of miles to people in faraway villages, and saved many lives.

Siberian huskies were first brought to Alaska to take part in sled races.

Growing Up

There's nothing as cute as a Siberian husky pup. But that little bundle of fur will soon grow into a lively dog that needs lots of attention.

A husky pup needs to be with her mom

and brothers and sisters until she is eight weeks old. Then she will be ready to go to her new home.

Be extra gentle at first while your little pup gets to know you.

Training Your Siberian Husky

The Siberian husky is smart and learns fast. She will be easy to train as long as she understands that you are in charge. The husky must see you as her pack leader or she may cause problems.

Huskies are friendly to everyone, so they do not make good guard dogs.

Always remember how much a husky loves to run.

Keep your dog on a leash when out and about.

Sled Dogs

Siberian huskies are the fastest of all sled-pulling dogs. They can average 14 miles an hour (22.5 km/h) and can run for hours.

One of the most famous sled dog races is the Iditarod Trail race, held in Alaska over several days during March.

Teams of 16 dogs race through blizzards and icy temperatures.

Working Huskies

The Siberian husky's bravery and intelligence make it a great search and rescue dog.

Huskies come from the north, but they have also been to the other end of the world. Explorer Richard E. Byrd took huskies with him on expeditions to the Antarctic.

A husky named Shadow helped in rescue work after the Oklahoma tornadoes in 1999. She helped her handler find many injured people in ruined buildings.

Your Healthy Husky

Huskies are healthy dogs, but they can suffer from hip problems. Find out as much as you can about your pup before buying and be sure to buy from a good breeder.

Your husky will shed lots of hair twice a year, so brush her coat every day at that time, and weekly at other times.

Check her ears, teeth, and nails often, too, and ask your vet if you have any worries.

Caring for Your Siberian Husky

Think carefully before buying a Siberian husky. She may live for 12-15 years, or even longer.

Every day your dog must have food, water, and exercise, as well as love and care. She will also need regular

checks and vaccinations. When you
go out or away on vacation, you will
have to make sure she is looked after.

If you care for your dog well,
she will be a happy, healthy
animal and bring you lots of joy.

Useful Words

breed
A particular type of dog.

Siberia
An area in the far north of Asia where the weather can be very cold.

vaccinations
Injections given by the vet to protect your dog against certain illnesses.

Index